FIVE MIDNIGHT MOMENTS

NEW YEAR BAE-SOLUTIONS

SHERYL LISTER

SL BOOKS

ABOUT FIVE MIDNIGHT MOMENTS

Some rules are meant to be broken.

A passionate affair with a sexy, charismatic man is right up Valencia Townsend's alley. Except when that man is her boss and it's against company policy. He may be irresistible, but she has no intentions of ending her year the same way it began - in a relationship headed nowhere.

The no-fraternization policy Dwayne Albright put in place to protect himself comes back to bite him with a vengeance. He never expected to meet Valencia, who completes him in every way. Now he has five nights—five moments—to decide whether to follow the rules or ring in the new year and every year with his perfect woman.

Five Midnight Moments Copyright © 2020
by Sheryl Lister
ISBN: 978-1-7338670-8-5
All rights reserved.

Editor: BR Sutton
Cover Design: Sherelle Green

For those who risk it all for love.

ACKNOWLEDGMENTS

My Heavenly Father, thank you for my life and for loving me better than I can love myself.

To my husband, Lance, you will always be my #1 hero!

To my children, family and friends, thank you for your continued support. I appreciate and love you!

To my writing tribe, thank you for being you.

Brandi, you are a lifesaver!! I love you.

To Ebony Evans and the EyeCU Group, thank you for sparking the idea!

Thank you to all the readers who have supported and supported me. I couldn't do this without you.

DEAR READER

Dear Reader ~

Have you ever heard the saying "some rules are meant to be broken? Valencia finds herself having to decide whether her relationship is worth that risk. And when Dwayne believes it is, midnight might just take on a whole new meaning. I hope you enjoy each moment!

Love & Blessings!
Sheryl

sheryllister@gmail.com
www.sheryllister.com

CHAPTER 1

*V*alencia Townsend shivered as she entered her condo and dropped her tote on a chair.

"Cold?"

She smiled. "Coming from those eighty-degree temperatures in Puerto Vallarta back to barely sixty here in Sacramento is enough to make anybody cold." She usually programmed the heating system, but when Dwayne Albright had asked her to go away with him for the weekend to Mexico as his Christmas gift, the only thing on her mind had been how fast she could pack. She walked over to the thermostat and cranked up the heat. "I wish we could've stayed longer," she said, rubbing her hands up and down her arms in an effort to warm up. After two and a half days of sunshine, pristine beaches and sumptuous foods, she loathed having to return to the real world.

Dwayne left her suitcase next to the sofa and wrapped his arms around her. "So do I. We'll have to do it again in the new year. I can't ever remember enjoying a trip so much."

"Neither can I."

He nuzzled her neck. "I especially liked that moonlit

beach walk." Tilting her chin, he stared at her intently. "I will never forget the kisses we shared, the passion in your eyes when we made love."

Her body heated with the remembrance. She wouldn't either. It had been the first time since they'd started dating four months ago that they could be seen together freely, which was part of her concern. Valencia backed out of his hold.

He frowned. "What's wrong?"

She pasted a smile on her face. "Nothing. I'm fine."

Dwayne viewed her skeptically, obviously not believing a word she said. "It's not *nothing*. You don't think I know when something's bothering you?" He closed the distance between them. "Tell me what's going on, sweetheart."

"Dwayne, I really like being with you, but I'm tired of hiding and I don't know how much longer I can do this." She scrubbed a hand across her forehead. The only person who knew about Valencia's relationship with Dwayne was her best friend, and she'd sworn Leah Ward to secrecy. She'd only told her friend that they worked together. Valencia hadn't even shared his name.

He sighed. "I know. It's hard on me, too."

"I want to be able to go to a movie or out to dinner without having to drive miles away. Or go out to lunch with you occasionally like regular couples do."

"So what are you suggesting?"

Valencia threw up her hands. "I don't know. Maybe we should just…end things before it's too late and start the new year as friends. Sooner or later, someone is going to see something and—"

Dwayne silenced her with a kiss. "Is that what you really want? To end things between us? Because I don't. We both knew what we were getting into when we started this relationship."

"No, I don't," she said softly. He was everything she could ask for in a man—intelligent, compassionate, hard-working, and a sexy hard rock body that belied the fact that he sat behind a desk all day. All six-foot plus inch of his coffee-with-cream colored body had called to her from the moment they'd met. And his smile made her weak...*every* time. But he was also her boss. The year was almost over and she was about to end it the same way it started—in a relationship headed to nowhere. Albright Financial Group had a no-fraternization policy, and sleeping with the man whose family issued her paycheck definitely topped the list of what not to do. She'd only worked there for six months and would be the only one at risk of losing her job.

"Baby, don't you know how much you mean to me?"

She figured he cared about her—the way he treated her said so. But did she really know how he felt? Sure, he'd thrown out those three little words in the throes of passion, but she had yet to hear them in the light of day. On the other hand, Valencia knew exactly how she felt about him. She'd fallen in love with Dwayne.

He palmed her face. "I don't want to lose you, Lyn."

"I don't want to lose you, either, but I can't see any way for this to work."

"It can, and it will. Trust me. You mean everything to me." Dwayne slanted his mouth over hers, kissing her deeply and seemingly trying to communicate just what that meant.

Her arms slid up the hard wall of his chest and circled around his neck. She moved closer to him and heard his deep groan. Every stroke of his tongue pushed her doubts further and further away, until nothing remained except *him* and the pleasure he always delivered. It was her turn to moan when he pulled her against his rigid erection. His hands roamed over her body, singeing her in every spot he touched. Valencia didn't realize he'd unbuttoned her blouse until she felt the heat of his tongue on the tops of her breasts. "Dwayne," she whispered.

"Yeah, baby."

"I thought you said on the plane that you had some work to do tonight."

Dwayne chuckled. "It can wait. Right now, my focus is on you." He swept her into his arms, strode down the hallway to her bedroom and placed her on the bed. His eyes never left hers as he stepped back and removed his clothes and donned a condom.

He came back to the bed and slowly finished undressing Valencia, kissing and licking his way up her body. Desire raced through her body and she trembled as his tongue made sweeping, swirling motions inside her mouth. He brought his hands up to frame her face, holding her in place and delving deeper. Without breaking the seal of their mouths, Dwayne shifted their bodies and guided himself slowly, inch by incredible inch, inside her. They both groaned.

He held himself still. "You said you wanted to start fresh in the new year. I want what you want—a fresh start, but with us. Together. That means I have five days, five nights to prove to you that what we have is more than an affair."

Valencia gasped when he withdrew and thrust deep inside her. She wanted more, too. She just didn't see it happening. But for now, tonight, she'd savor this time with him.

～

Monday morning, after the weekly staff meeting, Dwayne knocked on his brother's office door.

"Come in."

He entered and dropped down in the chair across from Dwight's desk. "How are you settling in?"

"I don't know how you wear these damn suits every day. These things are giving me hives." Dwight frowned and tugged at his already loosened tie. Until two weeks ago, he'd worked with a buddy in his construction business and preferred working outdoors to being cooped up in an office every day. He also tended to be more intense and bordered on being an introvert, a direct contrast to Dwayne's laid back and outgoing personality.

He chuckled. "You'll get used to it." Dwayne loved the world of money and investments and had followed in their father's footsteps with business and finance degrees—and had worked at the family firm since age eighteen—but Dwight opted for construction engineering. Of course, their father hadn't been too happy about Dwight's refusal to join the firm upon graduating from college, but to appease him, he had minored in finance. It had taken a full year after Reginald Albright's retirement for Dwight to relent, and Dwayne knew his brother had only stepped in to help him.

"I don't want to get used to it," he grumbled, leaning back in his chair. "Anyway, I've been checking out all the accounts and noticed a few irregularities in one."

"That's why I'm glad you're here. If anyone can find out what's going on, it's you. The security analyst is adding another layer of protection that should be done today or tomorrow, so I'm hoping any funny business will be easier to flag." They'd just acquired two big accounts and the last thing Dwayne needed was money to start disappearing from any of their client's accounts. Albright Financial Group prided themselves on being one of the best investment firms in the country and he had no intentions of letting someone ruin that reputation.

"Like I said, it looks like just the one account has been touched and only a hundred dollars is missing." Dwight drummed his fingers on the desk. "It's almost as if whoever is doing this is testing the waters to see if he or she can get away with it."

"I don't care if it's one cent, when I find out who the thief is, they're gone." Dwayne's cell buzzed. He dug it out of his pocket and smiled. "Hey, Leticia."

"Hey, stranger. Long time no see and I haven't talked to you in months."

"It's been a busy year. What's up?"

"I've got an invitation to a New Year's Eve party and thought maybe you could come along as my date. We could catch up. I hope you don't have any plans."

"Actually, I do. Sorry," he said. He planned to ring in the new year with only one woman. "I'm sure we'll catch up at my parent's New Year's dinner party." Their families had been friends for years and she and his sister, Shelby, were best friends.

"Probably," Leticia said, sounding disappointed. "I'll let you get back to work."

"Okay. See you later."

As soon as he disconnected, Dwight said, "You know she has it bad for you."

"What? We've been friends since we were kids and I think of her as another sister. She knows that." At age thirty-one, Leticia was the same age as his sister and five years his junior. He'd sensed some interest on her part the last few times he'd seen her, but had been careful not to do anything to give her the impression that he saw her as anything other than a friend.

"That may be true for you, but I talked to Shelby yesterday and apparently, you haven't made that clear enough because, from what I understand, Leticia was shopping for some outfit guaranteed to get your attention."

Dwayne groaned and scrubbed a hand down his face. "I don't need this right now."

Dwight shrugged. "What the problem? She's a nice woman, pretty, and you know she isn't trying to get with you for your money. It's not like you're dating anyone else at the moment."

"That where you're wrong. I've been dating someone for the past four months." And he couldn't tell a soul. Not until he figured out a way to ensure Valencia wouldn't be penalized.

His brother frowned and sat up straight. "Why haven't you said anything? You never mentioned one thing about her and I should at least know her name."

"It's complicated." He and Dwight were close and usually confided in each other about everything, but not this time. Dwayne had put the no-fraternization policy in place at the beginning of the year when he took over as CEO and a female employee wouldn't take no for an answer. After she ignored his polite, but firm refusals and he found her naked in his office, he'd fired her and issued the memo the next day. Now there was Valencia, who, like him tried to follow the rules and ignore their attraction. But the chemistry between them was too strong to resist and the past four months with her had been the best of his life. Thoughts of their conversation from the previous night surfaced in his mind. He couldn't lose her.

"What the hell kind of trouble are you in?"

"Nothing I can't handle." He stood. "I'll see you later. Let me know if you find anything else." Not bothering to wait for a response, he walked out. Dwayne knew he should go straight to his office two doors down, but his steps took him to the other side of the floor where Valencia's office was located. He knocked on her partially open door and saw her talking to the marketing manager. Shawna Baker had been with the company for two years and her skills had kept them firmly in the public's eye. "Good morning, ladies. Do you have a minute, Ms. Townsend?"

Valencia nodded. "Sure."

"We'll talk later, Valencia," Shawna said, heading for the door. "Mr. Albright." She gave him a coy smile and exited. Dwayne closed the door behind her and quietly turned the lock.

Valencia slowly rose to her feet. "Um...is something wrong? Did something happen with the security system? I mean we don't... you—"

"Relax, baby," he said softly. "I just needed to see you." They had agreed not to seek each other out or have any conversation outside of what was necessary for business. He'd been fine with that until he realized what he felt for her went far beyond a casual hookup. Dwayne loved everything about her, from her enchanting smile, dark brown eyes and sexy, petite curves to her rich vanilla bean coloring, which matched the sweet, soft scent she always wore. Even now, the naked desire he saw in her eyes nearly did him in. "You have no idea how hard it is for me to stand here and not take you in my arms." Dwayne didn't care about policies or rules right now. He just wanted her. Closing his eyes, he mentally counted to ten, trying to maintain his control, but lost the battle within seconds. He walked over to the desk where she stood.

"Whatever you're thinking, it's not a good idea." She tried to take a step back, but ended up against the desk. "I can't lose this job."

He angled his head thoughtfully. "Actually, it's the best idea I've had all day and there's no chance of you losing your job. I promise." He slid an arm around her waist, lowered his head and kissed her sensually, tangling his tongue with hers. Yeah, this was the best idea he'd had. Dwayne switched their positions so that she was standing between his legs. He deepened the kiss and brought their bodies closer. Her taste was like an aphrodisiac and he couldn't get enough.

Valencia moaned. Her eyes snapped open and she gasped. She jumped away from him so quickly, she almost lost her balance. "You should go."

"Probably, because right now I want to strip you naked, lay you on that desk and show you—"

Her eyes widened and she clapped a hand over his mouth. "Go," she whispered, glancing over her shoulder to the still closed door.

He took her hand and pressed a kiss in the center of her palm. She snatched her hand away and he chuckled. "I'll talk to you later." Dwayne held up five fingers. "Five nights." As he made his way back to his office, he smiled. It was time to put his plan in action.

CHAPTER 2

*V*alencia tried to concentrate on finishing up the last test on the new security protocol, but had difficulty. She still couldn't believe what Dwayne had done. He'd walked out of her office calm and in control, as if nothing had happened. She, on the other hand, had been left in a state of arousal that refused to die down. She briefly toyed with marching over to his office and giving him a taste of his own medicine, but figured they'd already tempted fate enough for one day. It would be just her luck for someone to barge in and find them in the middle of a heated kiss. Or worse—them half naked and her straddling him in his chair.

Shaking off the errant thought, Valencia turned her attention back to the program. By late afternoon, everything ran as expected. Whenever someone logged into a client's account, it would alert upper management and they would be able to track it and trace it back to the person's computer. She assumed, with the recent acquisition of two major clients, the company didn't want to take any chances. She sent Dwayne an email letting him know everything was in place. He replied almost immediately: *Thank you. I appreciate your hard work.* Impersonal. The part of her that had fallen for him felt a little disappointed. However, the rational part of her said she couldn't have it both ways.

She checked her emails one last time before preparing to shut down for the day.

"Valencia. Good, you're still here."

Valencia turned to find one of the administrative assistants standing in the doorway. Hey, Jenice. You just caught me. Is there something you need?" She really hoped not. It was already after five and Valencia should've been gone ten minutes ago.

"You had a delivery."

Puzzled, she locked her desk and slung her purse over her shoulder. "Since I'm leaving, I'll just follow you out and pick it up on my way out." She couldn't imagine who'd be sending her a delivery at work.

Jenice rounded her desk and pointed to a large vase that held a dozen red roses. "These are yours." She picked up a small teal gift bag and held it out. "This is a Tiffany's bag. Whoever he is, he's a keeper," she said with a smile.

Valencia gasped softly. It took several seconds for her to find her voice. "Um…yes, he is." The vase sat in a carrier box, which would make it easier for her to take in the car. She didn't dare open the card or the gift, even though she could tell by the look on Jenice's face, the woman was itching for some information. "Thanks. I'm going to take these gorgeous flowers home. See you in the morning."

"Have a good evening."

A few minutes later, seated in her car, Valencia opened the card. It only had two words and signed with his initial: *Tonight. Midnight. D.* "What does that mean?" she mumbled. She mentally went over their earlier conversation for any indication of what the cryptic words meant, but drew a blank. Setting it aside, she dug the small jewelry box out of the gift bag. Her heart raced as she opened. "Oh. My. Goodness." Inside, she found a diamond tennis bracelet with a diamond-encrusted 'V'. Leaning back against the seat, Valencia closed her eyes. If she wasn't already in love with Dwayne, this would have pushed her over the edge. He'd asked for five nights to prove their relationship meant more than a passing fling, that it was worth the risk. Obviously, he planned to go all out. She opened her eyes, started the car and drove off.

As soon as she got home, her cell rang. Valencia hurried over to the coffee table and set the vase down, the dug her phone out of her purse. She smiled when she saw Leah's name on the display. "Hey, girl."

"Don't 'hey, girl' me," Leah said. "You were supposed to call me last night when you got home."

Laughing, Valencia walked to her bedroom and deposited her purse and the gift bag on her dresser. "I know, and I'm sorry. I had planned to, but D—...um, he stayed around for a while and it was too late to call by the time he left." She groaned inwardly. Leah's middle name was *nosy*, and one slip and the woman would know everything about Dwayne Albright from his vital statistics to where he went to preschool.

"Mmm hmm. More like y'all got busy."

She dropped down on the bed, but didn't comment. As usual, Leah was spot on.

"That silence says I'm right. Did you talk to him about ending things like you mentioned?"

"Yes, but he wasn't on board with it at all. He wants to prove we can make it work." She kicked off her shoes.

"Aw, that's so romantic. Wait. Don't tell me he expects you two to keep your relationship a secret indefinitely."

"I don't know what he expects, but he showed up in my

office today. I thought he came to talk work, but he...he kissed me."

Leah screamed into the phone. "That's what I'm talking about! Looks like your mystery man is ready to come out of the shadows," she added with a giggle.

"Or something." She debated on whether to tell Leah about the gifts, and before she could stop herself, blurted out the words. "He had flowers and a bracelet from Tiffany's delivered before I left the office this evening." Her friend was silent for so long, Valencia thought they'd gotten disconnected. "Leah, are you still there?"

"I'm here. Sis, I think you're going to have to decide real soon what you want to do. Any man sending those kinds of gifts to the office of a woman he's not supposed to be seeing says he's serious about you."

She'd had the same thoughts and it scared her to death. At age thirty-three, she had almost given up hope of meeting a man like Dwayne—a man good to her and good *for* her. But would it cost her the job that she'd grown to love? "What if we go public, then a month or two later, he decides I'm not who he wants anymore? Everybody's going to know and think I'm trying to sleep my way to a better position."

"Relax, Lyn. For what it's worth, I just don't see him doing that. From what you've told me, which hasn't been much, he seems like a great guy."

"He is a great guy and I really like being with him." The past four months with Dwayne had been amazing and truthfully, she didn't want it to end.

"There you go. Think about it, your job isn't the only one at risk. His is, too."

"I doubt it," Valencia mumbled. It wouldn't even cause a blip on any radar since the man owned the company, but she couldn't tell her friend that. At least not yet.

"It'll work out," Leah said. "Anyway, tell me about your weekend in the sun."

She laughed. "It was amazing. Eighty-degree temperatures, miles of beautiful sandy beaches, and—"

"And a sexy ass man to help you get your freak on."

"Yep, that, too. A girl could really get spoiled. The great thing was that because he has a friend with a private jet, we didn't have to spend half of our getaway waiting in an airport."

"Spoiled indeed. Does he have any brothers?"

"He mentioned having a brother and a sister, but since we've been keeping the relationship on the down low, we haven't talked a lot about our families." Admittedly, Valencia had been curious about his family and whether they were a close-knit bunch. She'd only seen Dwayne's father because the older man's photo happened to be on the website.

"So, I guess that means you don't know if the brother is single."

She chuckled. "No, and I'm not asking."

"See, you just ain't right. I thought you were my BFF. Out here finding yourself a good man and won't even hook a sistah up," Leah grumbled.

"Whatever, crazy woman." Her stomach growled. She'd been so out of sorts after Dwayne left her office that she hadn't been able to eat much at lunch. "I need to get off this phone and find some food. I'm starving." And she wanted to call Dwayne to ask about that note.

"Okay, but you'd better keep me posted. And you could at least tell me the brother's name now."

"Soon."

Leah's heavy sigh came through the line. "Fine."

Smiling, Valencia shook her head. They'd been best friends since high school and there had never been a dull moment with Leah around. "I'll talk to you later." After disconnecting, she went to the kitchen and rummaged through the refrigerator for something quick and easy. Because she hadn't gone grocery shopping, she didn't find much and settled on canned chicken noodle soup and a turkey sandwich. While the soup warmed, she sent Dwayne a text.

A few minutes later, he replied: *You'll find out at midnight.*

Valencia: *Does that mean you're coming over at midnight, calling...what?*

Dwayne: *LOL! You'll have to wait and see.*

She sighed in frustration, then typed back: *Fine! Be like that.*

Dwayne: *I will.*

She tossed the phone on the counter. "I can't stand him." A lie, of course, but she'd never had patience when it came to surprises. Valencia couldn't do anything about it, so she sat at the table and ate while sifting through her mail.

Afterwards, she lit candles, turned on some smooth R&B and took a leisurely bubble bath. By the time she got out, she felt relaxed and sleepy. She glanced at the clock on the nightstand and noted that she had a little over an hour to go before midnight. Valencia made herself comfortable on the bed, turned on the TV and channel surfed for a few minutes before deciding on an old rerun of *Criminal Minds*. She couldn't go wrong with Shemar Moore on the screen. Halfway through the second episode, her doorbell rang, startling her. Forcing herself not to run, she clicked off the TV, made her way to the front door and saw Dwayne through the peephole. She unlocked it and let him in. "Hey."

"Hey, sweetheart." Dwayne placed a soft kiss on her lips and shut the door behind him.

"What's in the bag?" Valencia pointed to the small duffel on his shoulder.

He grinned. "Patience, baby." He reached for her hand, led her to the living room and gestured for her to sit on the sofa.

She sat and he lowered himself next to her. He had such a serious expression on his face, her heart began to pound. Valencia had been the one to suggest they end things, but knew it wasn't really what she wanted. Dwayne had told he didn't, either. Now, she couldn't be sure. "What is it?"

Dwayne tucked a strand of her hair behind her ear. "Nothing. I know you're curious about why I chose this time."

"I am."

A smile tilted the corner of his mouth. "Do you remember our first kiss?"

She lifted a brow. "Is that a trick question? I'm a woman. What do you think?"

Chuckling, he shook his head. "I know you do, and so do I. It was a warm August day and we'd driven to Lake Tahoe. When I brought you home that night, it was midnight. The kiss we shared hit me in a way I'd never experienced and I knew I had to find a way to keep you in my life. It was the beginning of everything beautiful and I thought it would the perfect time to remind you why we belong together."

Emotion clogged her throat and she didn't know what to say. Not only had he remembered their first kiss, but he'd also given it a special place in his memories. "Dwayne." She drew in a deep breath. He fingered the bracelet on her wrist. "Thank you for this. It's beautiful, and so are the roses."

His gaze briefly strayed to the flowers, then back to her. "And so are you." He reached into the duffel he'd placed on the floor next to him, withdrew another small teal box and handed it to her.

Valencia smiled. "You're really laying it on thick."

Dwayne shrugged. "Open it."

Inside, she found another charm, this one a diamond

crown. "This is…it's amazing." She leaned over and kissed him. "Thank you."

"I wanted you to know that you're my beautiful Black queen and I cherish you. I also thought it was fitting in light of the set down you gave Ingram a couple of months ago. I wanted to bow at your feet."

She laughed through the tears that flowed down her cheeks. Fifty-something year-old Ingram Fields had worked for the firm almost from its inception and had a bad habit of lording it over everyone. He thought he knew everything and had tried to challenge Valencia on her adding security measures, stating he'd managed several millions of dollars over the years fine and didn't feel her protocols were necessary. She'd asked the man pointed questions to which he'd had no answers, then told him he should focus on his job and leave hers alone. After the meeting, more than one person had come up to her to thank her for finally putting Ingram in his place. "You know he still doesn't talk to me."

"But you got the job done and I appreciate everything you've done to make our client's accounts safer. Now, my queen, it's time for your royal treatment."

"What are you talking about?"

"All queens deserve to be pampered and because you're mine, it's even more true. Let me show you how much I adore you." Dwayne picked up the bag, stood and extended his hand.

Valencia didn't hesitate. Taking his hand, she led him to her bedroom. She reached for his shirt, but he stilled her hands.

He shook his head. "This night is all about you, Lyn."

He slowly stripped away the lounging pajamas she wore, kissing each newly bared area until she lay flat on the bed. Moans spilled from her lips.

"Turn over," he whispered.

She complied and he trailed his tongue down her spine. He kissed his way back up to her neck, causing her to tremble.

"Don't move." Dwayne left the bed for a moment and stripped down to his black boxer briefs.

She waited for him to finish, but instead, he reached into the bag for something, then came back to the bed and straddled her.

"What are you doing?" Valencia glanced over her shoulder and tried to see what he held, but he blocked her view. A few seconds later, she felt something cool drip onto her back.

"Enjoy."

Before she could say anything, Dwayne's hands moved over her in a combination of deep, light and featherlike touches that lulled her into a state of total relaxation. He kneaded her shoulders, back and buttocks. His hands went lower, grazing her core and she moaned, wanting more. But he continued to massage her thighs, legs and feet. Valencia's breathing slowed and she felt herself drifting off. His deep voice near her ear awakened her.

"This is what you can look forward to in the new year— me taking care of you, just like a queen deserves. Tell me you want it as much as I do."

"Yes," she managed to say. No man had ever touched her as if she were a priceless work of art. She'd be crazy not to want what he offered. He turned her over and began again.

Dwayne brushed a kiss over her lips. "I'm glad to hear it."

Her eyes drifted closed once more as she gave herself up to the delightful sensations. She had no idea how much time passed, but when her eyes opened again, she found Dwayne fully dressed and staring intently at her.

"Sleep well, my beautiful queen. I'll see you in the morning." He covered her mouth in a slow-as-molasses kiss that made her want to strip him naked and treat him to the same sensual explorations. He slid off the bed. "I'll lock the door behind me."

She was glad because she couldn't move if her life depended on it. "Good night and thank you," she said, her voice slightly slurred. A couple of minutes passed and Valencia heard the click of the front door. The man didn't play fair. A smile curved her lips. *And I don't even care.*

CHAPTER 3

*T*uesday evening, Dwayne spotted Dwight seated at a small table in the crowded bar and grill, and started in that direction. "Hey," he said, sliding onto the opposite stool. Almost immediately, a server approached. "I'll have a White Russian, please."

She gave him a smile. "Coming right up."

"You're working later these days." Dwight tilted the beer bottle to his lips and took a swig.

"It's the end of the year, so there are several reports that need to get done. But you wouldn't know that since you never leave that office. I don't think one person even knows you work at the firm." How Dwight managed to slip in and out of the building unseen never failed to amuse Dwayne.

"I don't know how long I'm staying. I only came on board because you asked, but I'm still taking care of things at the construction company. The good thing is because of the weather, things are slower and Terrell can handle most of it alone." Dwight and Terrell Murray had been best friends since college and both had worked in construction. When Terrell proposed starting his own construction company three years ago, Dwight hadn't hesitated in signing on.

"Have you talked to Dad?"

"No, but I will. I'll be here until you find out who's trying to steal from the company. But it's not like you need my help. You're every bit the troubleshooter I am."

"That may be true, but I do need your help." Dwayne could easily track down the culprit on his own, but he wanted it done in secret, something impossible with his administrative assistant having access to his computer. "No one knows what you're doing except me. They'd find out if I started investigating them."

"Your drink, sir." The server placed the glass in front of Dwayne. "Can I get you anything else?"

"No, thank you." He waited until the young woman walked away before continuing his conversation. "How are you doing really?"

Dwight gave him a small smile. "How did I know you were going to ask that? I'm good, just like I told you the last hundred times you asked. It's been three years and I've moved on." He took a long drink from the bottle.

He studied his brother. After losing the woman who'd been one of his best friends and whom he had never had the chance to tell of his love, Dwight had become almost a recluse. Dwayne had felt his brother's pain as if it were his own. Only in the last few months had Dwight began venturing out again.

"And stop looking at me like that."

"That's what big brothers do."

Dwight snorted. "Big brother, my ass." They shared a smile. "So, what's up with this woman you're supposed to be dating. You've never been this closed-mouthed about a relationship before and I don't see why it's complicated. Either you're dating her or not.

He idly stirred the cream in his drink, then took a small sip before answering. "It's complicated because she works at the firm, and there a no frat policy." One that he regretted putting into place.

"Since when? I don't recall Dad having any rules about dating and I know for a fact that a couple of folk who work there are married."

"He didn't. I put it in place at the beginning of the year."

"I bet you're regretting it now," Dwight said with a chuckle.

"No shit." He took another gulp of his drink.

"Why now? Did you have some harassment issues between the employees?"

"Just one." Dwayne shared the details of what happened. "I fired her and sent the memo out the next day. But this is different. *She's* different, and I have no idea how to make this work. She's worried about losing her job and I can't let that happen."

He shook his head. "Come on, bro. It's simple. You're the boss and you have the final say on *all* matters. Change the damn rule." Dwight fell silent for a moment. "If you care about her, don't wait. You don't want to end up where I am," he added softly.

Dwayne contemplated the advice. No, he didn't want to end up in that same place. Though Elena had passed away from complications of Leukemia, if he lost Valencia, he imagined the loss would feel the same. "You're right, I don't."

"Who is she?"

"You'll find out soon enough." Tonight would be the second night of his plan and by the time New Year's Day came around, he intended for everyone to know. He decided to change the subject. "Let's order dinner and you can tell me how you plan to get Dad over to your side."

Laughing, Dwight said, "By doing the same thing I did the

first time—outright telling him I'm going back to construction."

Over dinner they laughed and talked about everything. Both had been so busy that it had been over two months since they'd hung out together and Dwayne missed him. He had a couple other buddies, but he was closest to his brother. Once they finished eating, the two lingered over their drinks a while longer before going their separate ways.

Dwayne showered when he got home, then spent time catching up on his personal and business emails. By the time he glanced up, it was time to leave. He grabbed the small gift bag and drove over to Valencia's house. He rang her doorbell at exactly midnight. When she opened the door and smiled at him, he knew he'd be changing that policy, sooner rather than later.

"Hey, handsome. Come on in."

"Hey, baby." He lifted her in his arms and kicked the door closed. "I missed seeing you today." He slanted his mouth over hers and immediately tangled his tongue with hers, wanting to absorb her taste into every fiber of his being. Whether coincidental or by design, every time he sought her out, she'd been away from her desk.

Valencia laughed. "Serves you right for what you did to me yesterday. Leaving people all hot and bothered. You're lucky I didn't come to your office and do you the same way," she added with a roll of her eyes.

Smiling, Dwayne wiggled his eyebrows. "Any time you want to come to my office, just let me know. I'll be waiting and ready."

She playfully punched him in the chest. "Whatever." He carried her over to the sofa and sat with her in his lap. "You know I kind of like these midnight rendezvous. It's sexy and the gifts have been out of his world." She fingered the bracelet.

"I agree. Every one of these midnight moments are aimed at keeping you by my side. Speaking of gifts…" He held up the bag.

"Dwayne, you don't need to buy me things to show you care."

"I know, but humor me, please."

Valencia accepted the bag, took out the small box and opened it. "A compass charm?"

"Yes. It means past, present, future…infinity. I drifted in and out of relationships looking for my right woman and my heart's compass led me to you." He'd never bared his soul to a woman before and had to pause to steady his emotions. "As long as you're with me, I'll never be lost. And I want to be the compass for your heart from now on."

She wiped the tears from her cheek. "You're killing me here. I've never cried so much in my life. I don't know what to say."

Dwayne used the pad of his thumb to swipe away a lingering tear. "It's easy. Say you'll stay on this journey with me, that we'll keep having our moments." When she opened her mouth to speak, he placed a finger on her lips. "Not yet. I have three more days. Right now, I want to do something I couldn't a couple of weeks ago at the firm's holiday party."

"What?"

"Dance with you." He stood and placed her on her feet. In the eighteen years he'd worked at Albright, he hadn't cared one bit about dancing, but watching Valencia with a few of the male employees almost made him lose his mind. The songs had all been up tempo, but the jealousy he'd felt didn't care. He took out his phone. searched for the song he wanted and hit the "play" button. Eric Benét and Tamia's *Spend My Life With You* flowed into the room and he pulled Valencia into his embrace. She rested her cheek on his chest and he heard her soft sigh.

"I wanted to dance with you, too," Valencia said, wrapping her arms around his waist. "I had a hard time ignoring you all night."

"Ditto." He rested his head on the top of hers, closed his eyes and swayed in time with the music. The lyrics expressed exactly how he felt—he wanted to spend his life with her. He'd been afraid of what she might say earlier and wanted her to wait until his days were up. Until he'd spoken every word that lay in his heart. Valencia lifted her head and stared up at him. She didn't say anything. She didn't have to. He heard her loud and clear, and he wanted the same thing. She came up on tiptoe and kissed him, tasting and teasing. The sound of her low moans in his ear and the way she returned his kiss with equal fervor fueled his passions, and he grew harder with each sensual moment. Without breaking the seal of their mouths, he strode down the hallway to her bedroom and lay her on the bed. After undressing them both and donning a condom, Dwayne took his time kissing, stroking and touching every part of her body, lingering on her round breasts, the sweet curve of her hips and her toned thighs.

"Dwayne," she whispered.

He loved hearing her soft sounds of pleasure and the way she called his name. "What, baby?"

"I need you inside me."

"I'll give you everything you need, everything you want, but we're not going to rush this." He lowered his body on top of her hers, being careful not to place all his weight on her. His hand traveled down her left leg and back up her right to her center, where she was already wet. Her legs parted to give him access, and he used a finger to circle her clit. Her legs trembled and she opened wider. Dwayne slid one finger in, followed by another, moving them in a steady rhythm. She cried out and arched against his hand. A moment later, she screamed his name as she came. Dwayne withdrew his fingers, shifted his body and guided his erection inside her. Her tight walls tightened around him and he shuddered. He withdrew and plunged deep, swiveling his hips in fine, subtle, circling movements. She gripped his shoulders and raked her nails down his back, causing him to shudder.

"I love how you make love to me."

Dwayne groaned and kept up the measured pace as he watched the play of passion across her features.

Valencia dug her nails into the flesh of his back and she arched higher to take him deeper. "Don't stop."

The pressure of her holding him so snugly made him increase the tempo, delving deeper into her with each rhythmic push and she matched his fluid movements. He gripped her hips and ground his body into hers. Her body began to shake and he buried his face in her throat and held her tightly against him, needing to be as close and deep as he could when she came. As spasms racked her body, it triggered his own release and the climax shot through him with a force that left him weak and panting. "I love you." And he couldn't lose her, no matter what.

Valencia nearly sprinted up the steps to her office building. She had slept straight through her alarm clock, then her car wouldn't start and she'd had to call Uber. She glanced at her watch again. Fifteen minutes late. Her night with Dwayne had been something out of a fantasy and she'd planned to send him a text this morning to tell him that she didn't need five days to decide what she wanted. She wanted him, *all* of him—policy or no policy. But right now, she didn't have time to savor her memories. She needed to get her butt in her office and pray no one had noticed her tardiness. Valencia pushed through the doors and hurried toward the elevator, her heels clicking on the marble floors.

She jabbed the button. "Come on, come on," she muttered. The doors opened and a man barreled out, almost knocking her over and spilling his coffee down the front of her gray silk blouse. Valencia cursed under her breath. The man apologized profusely and she snatched the napkins he offered and stepped into the waiting car. She selected her floor and tried to blot the coffee stains from her top. This day couldn't get any worse.

As soon as the doors swished open, Valencia started down the hallway, but was intercepted by two security officers.

"Ma'am, you need to come with us," one of them said.

"I'm already late and I need to get to my office."

The second man gently took her arm and steered her in the direction of a private conference room. "The boss wants to see you *now*."

What could Dwayne want with her first thing? And why send security? He could've just as easily waited for her in her office...or his. They escorted her into the office and gestured for her to sit. She met Dwayne's cold eyes. A stark contrast from the previous night's passion.

"Ms. Townsend."

The deep voice that had been filled with so much emotion when he whispered in her ear last night now held none. "What's going on?"

Dwayne leaned forward. "You tell me. Last night one hundred and fifty thousand dollars of Mr. Smith's money has been diverted out of his account an into a dummy account linked to your computer."

Valencia was wrong. Her day had not only gotten much worse, it had just been shot to hell. "I didn't do this. And I was nowhere near my computer last night," she snapped. She had been with him, so she didn't understand why he was pretending not to know her whereabouts.

He lifted a brow. "No? The only person who's logged onto your computer in the last twenty-four hours is you. I have to hand it to you, you're good. We might not have ever found it had it not been for the new security system we put into place this week." He slid two photos across the table. "You didn't even bother to change clothes."

"You mean the one I put in place," Valencia corrected, her anger mounting. She snatched up the pictures and her blood ran cold. The first one had been taken earlier in the day after she'd returned from taking a walk on her break. The other one was time-stamped at 12:15 a.m. The woman in the photo had on an identical outfit, but a large hat and dark glasses obscured her face. She had no idea who the woman was, but Valencia knew it wasn't her. "This isn't me. And I have a solid alibi from midnight last night until five this morning. Remember?"

"Ms. Townsend, I have no idea what you're talking about or what I'm supposed to remember. All I know is you're fired and you have fifteen minutes to clear out your office."

Valencia leaped to her feet, leaned across the desk and pointed her finger in his face. "I don't know what kind of *sick* game you're trying to play, but I'm not going anywhere because I. Did. Not. Steal. *Anything!*" She'd spent all night and damn near all morning with this man and now he had the nerve to act like it never happened, but oh, *nooo*, she wasn't having it. Not today. Not ever.

Dwayne nodded toward the two officers and they grabbed her arms. "Please see Ms. Townsend out."

She struggled against the two men. "I'm not going anywhere until you tell the truth!" Valencia did her best to get away from them, but she was no match for their combined strength. She just wanted two minutes to rearrange Dwayne's face, then she'd gladly leave.

The door burst open. "What the hell is going on? Everybody on this floor can hear all this shouting."

If Valencia knew how to faint, she would have at that moment.

He fully entered the office and seemed to notice her for the first time. His eyes widened and then he frowned. "Dwight, why are they holding Valencia like that?"

Dwight? She divided her surprised gaze between the man still fuming behind the desk and the one who had just entered. "Dwayne?"

He smiled. "Of course. Baby, are you okay?"

"I'm…yeah." Their height, facial features and even the sounds of their voices were the same. Valencia shook her head in an attempt to clear her confusion and shifted her gaze back to Dwayne…or Dwight and waited while he explained the whole sordid tale again.

Dwayne shook his head. "She didn't do this, bro. Lyn was with me all night."

She snatched away from the men still holding her and glared at Dwight. "I told you I didn't do it. So, I'm guessing there should be some sort of apology on your part about now, right?" She folded her arms. "I'll wait."

Dwayne chuckled and turned to the two officers. "We can take it from here. Thanks." The men nodded and left, and he closed the door behind them. "Since we know Valencia didn't do it, we need to find out who did."

Fuming, Valencia said, "You'd better believe I will." She shifted her gaze to Dwight. "Still waiting on that apology *and* my job."

"My apologies, Ms. Townsend," Dwight said. "And you're good on the job front."

Sending him one more icy glare, she spun on her heel and

stalked across the room toward the door. Halfway there, she stopped, came back and snatched the photos off the desk. "When I find out who did this, it's gonna be on," she muttered.

Dwayne reached out and touched her arm. "Are you sure you're okay?"

"I've been accused of stealing from my employer, some crazy coworker is impersonating me, and I found out that your brother is actually your *identical twin*. Why wouldn't I be okay?" Her voice rose with every word, but she couldn't help it. She pushed past him and stormed out. A few people loitered in the hall and a couple stuck their heads out of their offices, no doubt curious about what had happened, but she didn't slow. Valencia had one goal—finding the person who had the audacity to impersonate her. And when she did…she was kicking somebody's ass.

CHAPTER 4

"*S*o *that's* who you're screwing."

Dwayne shot his brother a dark glare. "That's not how it is and you know it," he gritted out.

Dwight folded his arms. "So you're not screw—"

"If you say one more word, I swear I'm going to knock the shit out of you."

"You're really feeling her, aren't you?"

"I said that last night."

He laughed softly and shook his head. "She is something, though. What is she, five-two or three?"

"About that."

"I'm a foot taller and she didn't back down for one minute. She seriously looked like she was ready to do me bodily harm."

"You deserved it for the way you came at her."

Dwight shrugged. "Hey, the info came from her computer, what was I supposed to think? And if you'd told me last night who you were in a *relationship with*," he emphasized, "I would've known she didn't do it. And are you sure she was with you the entire time?"

Dwayne lifted a brow. "I got to her house at midnight and I didn't leave until five this morning, so yeah, I'm sure." It had been hard to leave her and the only reason he had was because he didn't have a change of clothes. He wouldn't make the same mistake again. "Now that we know Valencia didn't do it, we need to find out who did and get that money back quick."

"Whoever did it, used the computer in Valencia's office. The only thing we have to go on are the photographs. The woman was dressed the same."

"Someone's going through a lot of trouble, but why target Lyn?" he murmured. "She's only worked here six months and gets along with everyone. Well, except Ingram." At his brother's puzzled expression, Dwayne took a few minutes to explain how Valencia had put the man in his place during a staff meeting.

Dwight burst out laughing. "She does not play."

"Not at all. It took everything I had to keep a straight face. I think I fell in love with her that day."

His laughter faded. "Wait. You're in love with her?"

"Yeah, I am. She's everything I want in a woman—intelligent, tough, beautiful inside and out."

Dwight clapped Dwayne on the shoulder. "I'm happy for you, bro."

Dwayne stared at the face so like his own. "Thanks. I should probably go talk to her. I think she was a little pissed at me, too."

"Let me know how it goes. I'll be working on finding that money, although, I suspect Ms. Townsend might beat me to it. I'd hate to be in that person's shoes when she does."

"For real," he agreed. Another reason why he needed to check on her. "Let me know if you find something." He stood and left. On his way to her office, he racked his brain trying to figure out why someone would steal from the accounts.

Out of the thirty-five employees who worked at Albright Financial, twenty were women. He could rule out a few because of their height, but that still left far too many. He did not need this right now.

Dwayne poked his head in Valencia's partially open door. She sat at her laptop muttering under her breath and tapping the keys with such force, they'd cry for mercy if they could. If she kept it up, she might need a new keyboard soon. Clearly, she was still angry. He couldn't blame her because if someone had impersonated him to steal money, he'd be out for blood, too. He stood there watching her for a few more seconds before making his presence known. "How mad are you with me?"

"Still deciding," Valencia said, not taking her eyes off the screen.

"Hey, I'm not the one who accused you. In fact, I came to your rescue." He walked over to her desk and propped a hip on the corner. "The way I see it, I shouldn't be on your hit list."

She finally looked his way, her anger plain. "Why didn't you tell me you were a twin?"

Dwayne scrubbed a hand down his face. "No one was supposed to know we're dating, so I didn't really think it was an issue. And we really hadn't gotten into each other's family trees. I don't know much about your family, either, so, it's not fair for you to hold it against me," he added with a grin.

"I guess." A small smile peeked out. "Who's older?"

"Me, by five minutes. And I never let Dwight forget it. I'd actually had planned to tell you about him and my entire family this week," he said going back to their previous conversation.

"Why now?"

"Because I'm done with the secrecy." He also wanted her to meet the rest of his family, but decided not to share that piece of information just yet. He trailed a finger down her cheek and tilted her chin. "I'm done with all of it, Lyn." He placed a soft kiss on her lips. Dwayne could see the wheels turning in her mind and changed the subject. He gestured to her computer. "Find anything?"

Valencia stared at him, then said, "Not yet. Whoever she is, she's good. The files were accessed directly from my computer, so you can add breaking and entering to your list of crimes. I distinctly remember locking my office and Jenice can vouch for me because she'd stopped to ask if I'd gotten any more gifts."

His mouth settled in a grim line. Only two people had a master set of keys—him and his administrative assistant. No way would he believe Norma Roberts had anything to do with this. The forty-something woman had worked in the same position for over fifteen years, first with his father and now, Dwayne. On the way back to his office he was going to stop by Human Resources and pull a few files.

"I can't figure out why someone would target me. I've only worked here six months and, aside from Ingram—who can barely retrieve his password from a computer, let alone try to siphon money out of an account—I haven't had a run-in with anyone else."

"I'd wondered the same thing." The only other alternative was someone wanted to ruin him, the company or both. Dwayne had continued the same comfortable, family-oriented working environment as his father and got along with all the employees, so he didn't have a clue as to the reason why. Valencia touched his arm and drew him out of his thoughts.

"Hey. I'm going to find out who did this."

"I know. I'm going to look into a few things and Dwight is working on it, as well."

Valencia frowned. "Oh, great. I just thought of something."

"What is it?"

"I could've been smiling at Dwight some of those times I passed you in the halls."

She looked so mortified, he couldn't do anything but laugh.

"It's not funny, Dwayne."

"I can guarantee you he hasn't gotten any of my smiles. Dwight has only been here a couple of weeks and he rarely leaves the office."

"Thank goodness," she said, slumping against the chair. "Some of the thoughts I had—." She cut herself off and spun around back to her computer.

Dwayne rotated her back to face him, leaned down and braced his hands on the chair's armrests. "Naw, baby. I want to hear all about those thoughts. Maybe they're the same as the ones I've had about you."

"Um…we have a thief to catch right now, and didn't you say you needed to look into a few things?"

Sobering, he straightened and blew out a long breath. "Yeah, we do." He pressed a kiss to her forehead. "Let me know if you find something, and I'll do the same."

"Okay."

Because his father built his business during the days when paper ruled, Dwayne had the human resources manager pull the files he needed. However, he'd grown up in the world of technology, so he also kept electronic records. For the next several hours, he went through each file, making notes and flagging anything that could be considered a clue. He paid particular attention to those who had extensive computer experience.

When he came up for air, it was after three. His stomach growled and reminded him that he'd worked straight through lunch. Closing the files, Dwayne locked them in his file cabinet and went to the sandwich shop on the first floor.

He found Dwight waiting in his office when he returned. His heart rate kicked up. "What did you find out?"

"Nothing yet. I've been checking out the two women who work in marketing and the one in IT, since they have the most computer experience and wanted to ask you about them."

"What do you want to know?" He sat down at the small conference table on the other side of the office and unwrapped the turkey sandwich.

Dwight took the chair opposite him, opened Dwayne's bag of chips and dug out a few.

"You really need to stop grabbing people's stuff and get your own damn food." For as long as he could remember, Dwight always helped himself to someone's food or drink. Because they were twins, Dwayne ended up being his victim most often.

Smiling, he said, "You wouldn't know what to do if I stopped."

"Yes, I would. I'd be able to eat in peace." Dwayne slid the bag closer to him. "You wanted to ask some questions?"

"Yeah. How long has Ms. Lynch worked in IT?"

Before he could answer, Valencia stormed into the office with fury in her eyes and slapped a photo on the desk.

"It's Shawna."

"The marketing manager?" Dwight asked with a raised eyebrow.

Valencia nodded. She pointed to the photo of a woman sitting at Valencia's desk. "I recognize the bracelet she's wearing. She doesn't have gloves on and I guarantee you'll find her fingerprints on my keyboard or mouse."

Dwayne shook his head. "They'd probably be smeared since you've been on it today."

"I used my laptop today, not my computer. And every night, I wipe down the screen, keyboard and mouse."

He recalled her being on her laptop when he'd been in her office earlier. He walked over to his desk and hit the intercom. "Mrs. Roberts, can you please ask Shawna to come to my office?"

"Sure can."

He shared a look with Dwight, then turned toward Valencia. She looked ten times angrier than she had this morning. Not good. Dwayne thought about asking her to leave, but knew what her response would be, so he didn't bother.

"I'll call the police," Dwight said, taking out his phone.

Two minutes later, Mrs. Roberts escorted Shawna into the office.

Shawna smiled. "Well, this is an honor, Mr. Albright," she said, entering. "I've never been called to the bos—" Her eyes widened and she gasped when she noticed Dwight across the room. "Who is...what's going on?"

Dwayne's gaze dropped to her wrist. She had on the same multi-colored crystal bracelet from the photo. He sighed inwardly. "That's what I'd like to know. Would you like to tell me why you stole a hundred and fifty thousand dollars from one of our client's accounts and used Ms. Townsend's computer to do it?"

"I have no idea what you're talking about," she said, looking from one person to another.

Dwight held up the photo. "This says differently."

"That's not me!"

"*Lying bi—*" The rest of Valencia's words were drown out as she crossed the space in a flash, punched Shawna in the face, knocking her on her butt. The woman lost a shoe in the process and her wig ended up slightly crooked. Pointing a finger in Shawna's face, Valencia said, "The next time you try to impersonate somebody, don't forget to take off that *loud ass bracelet!*"

Dwayne and Dwight stood in stunned silence, then Dwayne gently pulled Valencia back. "Let's try this again, Ms. Baker. Better yet, you can explain it to the police."

"*No!* I'll tell you everything and I can get the money back." Shawna scrambled off the floor, not bothering to fix her wig or retrieve her shoe and started singing like Jill Scott. She threw her cousin—the woman Dwayne had fired for harassment—under the bus and backed it over her, tearfully confessing how she'd paid Shawna to ruin him. The woman had been essentially blackballed and unable to find another job in her field, and was still angry because Dwayne had rejected her advances. Shawna also gave up the account information where the stolen money was supposed to be deposited. Fortunately, because of the immediate alert from the security system and Valencia's quick work, when they accessed the account, the money was still there and could be returned to its rightful owner .

Dwayne didn't have one ounce of sympathy and turned her over to the police, who said they'd be picking up Shawna's cousin for questioning, as well. A detective and a couple other officers stayed around to question them further and to collect any evidence from Valencia's office.

After all the commotion died down, he sat in his office with Dwight and Valencia as she worked to redeposit the money into Mr. Smith's account. His woman was something else. Not only had she solved the case in record time, she'd delivered a punch that would've made Muhammed Ali proud. She'd done it in a skirt and heels and not one strand of her shoulder-length hair was out of place.

Dwight stood. "I'll leave you two alone. Ms. Townsend, nice work."

"Thanks," Valencia said.

As soon as the door closed, Dwayne pulled her out of her seat and held her close. "Thank you."

"I'm glad she was so stupid. It made it easier. I guess I'm going to be fired for knocking her out."

"Hardly. It was justified and you saved Mr. Smith and the firm from a big loss. It's been a long day and it's almost seven. Why don't you go on home?" They'd had to endure almost two hours of questions from detective.

"Are you coming over tonight?"

"You'd better believe it. Midnight."

"I'll be waiting." She seemed to war with herself for a few seconds, then came up on tiptoe and gave him a quick kiss. "See you at midnight."

He smiled. She was definitely the one for him.

After a long bath and a glass of wine, Valencia finally felt her calm return. She couldn't believe a woman would be so upset about Dwayne saying no that she tried to ruin his entire career and get Valencia thrown in jail. Then again, if word got out, it could have affected everyone's job. She shook her head to push the rising anger down and went to refill her glass. The day had been so crazy, she'd forgotten about not having a car until she'd gotten ready to leave. By the time she made it home, the auto shops near her had all closed, which meant another Uber ride in the morning. She probably could have asked Dwayne to bring her home, but Valencia needed a few minutes to herself. She prided herself on being relatively even-tempered. Even when she'd issued the set-down to Ingram, she had done it with class and without raising her voice once. Today, however, a side she never knew existed surfaced and exploded in a matter of minutes.

Back in the living room, she sat on the sofa, reclined and

tossed the car manual on the end table. Hopefully, it would turn out to be nothing more than a dead battery. She still couldn't believe Dwayne had a twin. She'd studied them both and they were identical in every way. It took her a little while to find something to distinguish the brothers from each other, but she finally figured out how to tell them apart— their eyes. While both had the same shape and coloring, Dwayne's held a playful light that Dwight's lacked. His, on the other hand, had been shuttered and she saw what looked like sadness in their dark depths. She couldn't help but wonder what happened.

Valencia sipped her wine as her mind drifted to Dwayne's words. *I'm done with the secrecy.* Truthfully, so was she. Today, she'd kissed him in his office and it had been one of the boldest things she'd ever done. Unless she counted that punch to Shawna's jaw. She flexed her hand. It was still a little sore, but knocking her out felt so good. Needing to talk to someone other than Dwayne, she grabbed her phone and called Leah.

"Hey, girl," Leah said when she answered. "You calling to update me on your as-the-mystery-man-turns soap opera?"

Valencia laughed for the first time that day. "You are so crazy. I don't know how we've been friends all these years."

"Yes, you do. I'm the friend who's there to keep your otherwise bland life exciting. Although, I must admit, you've spiced it up a little these past few months. So, what's up?"

"I almost got fired today." She gave her friend a rundown of the day's events, but had to stop every other word because Leah was either screaming or cursing.

"I hope your boss is on top of things."

"We already found out who did it. Long story short, the woman was paid by a relative who'd been fired for sexual harassment. But I still have no idea why she used my computer, though."

"You should've called me so I could beat her ass because she deserves it. I know you wouldn't do it because you're too nice sometimes." Growing up, Leah had never been one to shy away from a fight. She may not have started them, but she always finished them.

"Not this time," Valencia mumbled.

"What does that mean?"

"She kept saying she had no idea what we were talking about and I got tired of her repeating that same lame lie, so I punched her in the face."

Leah burst out laughing. When she finally calmed down, she sniffed and said, "I'm so proud."

She couldn't say it was her proudest moment, but seeing Shawna sprawled on the floor had given Valencia some measure of satisfaction.

"Since your mystery man works there, I'm sure he heard about it. What did he have to say?"

For the millionth time, she debated on whether to tell Leah the truth. Once again, Dwayne's words floated through her mind. If he was okay with them going public, she could be, too, especially to her best friend. "He turned her over to the police."

"Wait. What?"

"My mystery man is Dwayne Albright, CEO of Albright Financial Group."

"You're dating your *boss*?" Leah screeched.

"Yep, and I have to go because he's coming over." They'd been talking for over two hours.

"You can't just drop that bomb on me and say you have to go. What kind of friend are you?"

"Your best friend."

"Valencia Denise Townsend, don't make me have to camp out on your doorstep to get answers."

"I won't, Leah Sheree Ward. Later, girlfriend." Valencia

could still hear her friend fussing as she disconnected. She finished off her wine and picked up the manual.

Like clockwork, Dwayne rang her doorbell precisely at midnight. When he entered, he didn't say anything, just wrapped her in his arms and held her close, as if he knew they both needed this. At length, he eased back.

"How are you doing?"

"I'm okay. You're the one I'm concerned about."

Dwayne gave her a small smile. "I have to say it's been a helluva day, but holding you in my arms makes everything better."

"I feel the same way." The kiss that followed was soft, sweet and filled with so much emotion, it brought tears to her eyes. When it ended, she rested her head against his chest. The rapid pace of his heart matched hers. She took his hand and led him to the living room.

He sat next to her on the sofa and gestured to the manual. "Is something wrong with your car?"

Valencia blew out a long breath. "Yeah. It wouldn't start this morning. With everything that went on today, I didn't get a chance to call the shop."

A frown creased his brow. "Then how did you get to work?"

"Uber."

"Baby, why didn't you call me? And this evening, you took Uber home, too? You know I would've taken you home."

She leaned her head against his shoulder and he wrapped his arm around her. "I know. But I needed some time and I know you had to do a few things, as well."

"Anything I had to do could've waited. Promise me you won't do this again."

The sincerity in his voice touched her deep inside. "I promise."

"Good. I'll check and see if I can find out what's wrong."

"Thank you."

"Now, for my next midnight moment." They shared a smile. He handed her yet, another jewelry box.

"I feel like it's Christmas all over again." This time, nestled against the black velvet, she found an anchor charm. "This is so beautiful and I have to say that diamonds are definitely becoming my best friend."

"The anchor symbolizes hope, security and stability, and you are all that and more for me. Today tested me in a way that I'd never experienced, but you kept me grounded. With you by my side, I felt calm in the face of that storm, as if nothing could shake my foundation. Let me do the same for you, baby. I want be your anchor, the one to keep you safe from whatever storms life throws in your path."

All she could do was nod around the lump in her throat. She'd been out of her mind to think she could give him up. Valencia cupped his clean-shaven cheek. "You are the most amazing man I have ever met." Leaning up, she kissed him and tried to communicate just how much she'd come to love him.

"You're the amazing one, sweetheart. I'd like for you to pack a bag. You're coming home with me. We're riding to work in the morning *together*. And before you say anything, I don't care what anyone thinks. We're grown and it's nobody's business what we do. So?"

She didn't even hesitate. "Give me ten minutes."

CHAPTER 5

*a*side from a few curious looks when Valencia and Dwayne arrived at the office together the next morning, no one said a word. She wouldn't have cared anyway because she was far too happy. Instead, they were still whispering about what had happened the previous day. With it being New Year's Eve, she hoped they could have their own private party. A smile curved her lips. She could think of nothing she'd rather do than spend another night in his arms.

At five o'clock on the dot, Valencia locked up and headed over to meet Dwayne. She said hello to Mrs. Roberts as she approached Dwayne's office.

The woman gave her a knowing smile. "Go on in, Valencia. He's expecting you."

"Thank you." She opened the door and saw Dwight sitting at the small conference table. He wore the same white dress shirt as Dwayne, but the moment he looked her way, she knew he wasn't the man she loved. "Oh, hey, Dwight. I was looking for Dwayne."

Dwight leaned back in the chair and studied her. "Not

many people are able tell us apart. Actually, no one usually does, except our mother. Yet, after one day, you can. How?"

Before she could answer, Dwayne came in. Valencia's heart fluttered in a way that it hadn't with his brother.

Dwayne gave her a quick kiss. "Hi, baby. Are you ready to leave?"

"Yes."

Dwight stood. "Seems like Valencia doesn't have a problem telling us apart."

"Really? I've been trying to get my mom to share her secret for years, and she won't."

She nodded. "Yep. And I'm not telling, either."

Dwayne folded his arms and a sexy grin spread across his lips. "Hmm, I think I may be able to persuade you to give up the goods."

Valencia divided a quick glance between the brothers and felt her face warm in embarrassment. "Um…I can just wait for you in the hall." Dwight's expression never changed and he had yet to crack a smile, so she had no idea what he was thinking.

He chuckled and walked over to his desk. "You don't need to leave." After powering off his computer, he locked everything and turned to Dwight. "How late are you staying?"

"I'm leaving right behind you."

"Okay. See you tomorrow."

Dwight nodded. "You two have a good evening."

"You, too," Valencia said. As soon as she and Dwayne got into his car, she said, "I don't think your brother likes me."

Dwayne laughed as he pulled out onto the road. "Quite the opposite. Yesterday, he told me I was lucky we're brothers, otherwise, he'd make a play for you."

Her head whipped around. "What?"

"Apparently, he was pretty impressed with the way you

handled Shawna, not to mention, the fact that you didn't back down when he thought you were the culprit."

She waved a hand. "That's...I mean how? He barely even talks to me."

"That's because he's more of an introvert. He barely talks to anyone, so don't take it personal. If he didn't like you, you'd know. *Trust me.*"

"If you say so," she said, staring out the window and rubbing her hands together. The early evening temperatures hovered around fifty degrees and she longed for the warm, sunny weather in Mexico.

Dwayne must have noticed her shivering because he said, "The heat will be up in a minute." They rode in companionable silence for a few minutes, then he spoke again. "I went out at lunch and got a new battery for your car."

"Aw, you're so sweet. Thank you, baby."

He smiled. "You're welcome."

After a couple more miles, she realized they weren't going in the direction of either of their homes. "Where are we going?"

"I thought we'd go out for dinner." He slanted her a quick glance. "In town."

She didn't know what to say. Over the past few days, he'd made a point of focusing on the things she wanted in a relationship. This would be the first time they'd be seen in public together. "Where are we going? With it being New Year's Eve, we might have problems getting a table."

"Not if we already have reservations."

For the past three nights, he'd been showing her in every way how much he cared about her. And when he said he loved her after they made love the last time, she'd felt it. Tonight would be her turn to tell him how much she loved him, too. The upscale steakhouse with its low lighting provided the perfect backdrop for lovers, but all she wanted at the moment was him. Preferably naked and buried deep inside her.

"You need to stop looking at me like that or we aren't going to be able to finish dinner."

Valencia gave him a sultry smile. "We could always take it to go."

Desire lit his eyes. "We could, but I have plans for us tonight, so eat your food and quit tempting me."

She slipped off her pump and slid her foot up his leg. "I have a few plans, too."

Dwayne choked on his wine. "Behave."

Giving him a mock pout, she said, "You're no fun."

"I'll give you all the fun you can stand later and that's a promise."

"Oh, alright." Dwayne made a point of whispering just what that fun entailed throughout the meal and the heat between them steadily rose. By the time he escorted her to the car, she was ready to straddle him right there in the back seat. With all the people milling around, she figured it wouldn't be a good idea, so she stifled the urge.

"What do your parents usually do on New Year's Eve?" Dwayne asked as he drove.

Valencia rolled her head in his direction. The question was so out of the blue, it caught her by surprise. "Um...the same thing they do every year—sit in front of the television waiting for the ball to drop in Times Square. Why?"

"I think it's time I met them. See if they're up for a visit."

She felt her eyes widen. "*Now*? You want to meet my parents tonight?"

Dwayne gave her that patented grin that make her weak and tossed her a bold wink. "Yep. So go ahead and make the call...unless there's some reason you don't want me to meet them."

"I...ah...no, there's no reason." Still staring at him and

trying to figure out what he was up to, she pulled out her phone and hit the call button next to her mother's name. She hadn't even told her parents anything about him other than they'd gone out a few times.

"Hey, baby girl," her father said when he picked up.

Valencia smiled. "Hi, Dad. Are you guys busy tonight?"

"Of course not. I hope this means you're coming by for a visit."

"That's the plan."

"Wonderful. We'll see you when you get here."

"I'm, um, bringing someone with me."

"Oh? A young man?"

She glanced Dwayne's way and he mouthed, "I'm not that young."

She playfully punched him. "Yes, Dad. We'll see you soon." Valencia ended the call and didn't know why she suddenly had a case of nerves. She told herself that this was the next natural step in their relationship and there was nothing to be nervous about. She was a thirty-three year-old woman, not a teenager. She gave Dwayne directions and when they arrived twenty minutes later, the butterflies continued to dance in her belly. She'd only introduced two guys to her parents and her father hadn't liked either of them. Dwayne kissed her temple, drawing her out of her musings.

"You'd think you're the one meeting my parents with the way you've been fidgeting," he teased. "If you're this nervous now, how are you going to be when I take you to meet my family tomorrow?"

Valencia eyed him. "Tomorrow?"

"They have a get-together every year on New Year's Day and it'll be the perfect time for you to meet everyone." Dwayne got out of the car and came around to help her out. He slung an arm around her shoulder and they started up the walkway. "Relax, sweetheart."

Evidently, her father had told her mother to expect them because the door opened before they got there. "Hey, Mom."

"Hi, honey," she said, barely sparing her a glance. "And who's this handsome young man?"

"This is Dwayne Albright. Dwayne, my mom, Norma Townsend."

Dwayne turned his megawatt smile on her mother. "Mrs. Townsend, it's an absolute pleasure to meet you."

"Please, come in." As they entered, her mother whispered to Valencia, "He's a cutie."

Valencia rolled her eyes at her mother giggling like a teenager. She had never seen her mother behave like this with the other guys she brought home, but then again, neither of them had been anywhere near as charming as Dwayne. Her father stood when they rounded the corner to the family room. "Hey, Dad." He engulfed her in a hug. "Dad, I'd like you to meet Dwayne Albright. Dwayne, this is my father, Raymond Townsend."

"It's good to meet you, Dwayne," her father said, shaking Dwayne's outstretched hand.

"The pleasure is mine, sir."

"You two have a seat."

They took seats on the sofa, while her parents reclaimed their favorite recliners.

"So, how long have you been dating and where did you meet?" her mother asked.

"We've been dating for four months and...we work at the same firm." Valencia hoped they wouldn't question further, but her mother's expression—the mama interrogation one—said otherwise.

"That's nice. How long have you worked there, Dwayne?"

"Eighteen years. I started right out of high school working summers and came on full-time after graduating college," Dwayne answered, seemingly unbothered by the scrutiny.

Her father peered over his glasses. "Are you in computer security, too, or finance?"

"Finance. Actually, I took over as CEO at the start of the year when my father retired."

Her mother gasped. "You're her boss."

"Yes, ma'am."

Valencia's parents shared a speaking glance that wasn't lost on her.

"How about I get us some dessert?" her mother asked, nearly jumping up from the chair. "Valencia, you can help me."

Norma Townsend's soft tone didn't fool Valencia one bit, and she knew her help wasn't optional. Dwayne seemed to sense the same thing and gave Valencia's hand a reassuring squeeze. She, reluctantly, got up and followed her mother into the kitchen. Valencia spoke before her mother could say anything. "Yes, I know I shouldn't have gotten involved with my boss, but it wasn't something either of us planned. It just happened."

"How long did it take for you two to...stop being professional?"

"Two weeks," she mumbled.

"Hmph. Two weeks?"

Oh, brother. Here we go. Valencia steeled herself for the lecture she knew was coming.

A grin played around her mother's mouth. "I can see why. It might've just *happened* to me, too, if I were in your place. And it would've taken me far less than two weeks."

Her mouth fell open. That was the last thing she expected her mother to say. "Mom?"

"What? I wasn't always this old. Just ask your father," she added with a sly wink.

They burst out laughing. Reason number two-hundred and fifty why she loved her mother.

~

Dwayne had no illusions about the hasty exit Mrs. Townsend made, and the look on her husband's face confirmed it.

"Most companies frown on those types of relationships," Mr. Townsend said.

No beating around the bush here. Just straight to the point. "True, and mine does, as well. However, your daughter is an amazing woman and as hard as we tried to keep things professional, it didn't work. I fell for her the first time we talked."

"What exactly does that mean?"

"It means I love her and I don't plan to let any policy dictate our relationship. I know you're concerned, but I promise that this won't affect her job in any way. Anyone who has something negative to say will have to go through me." He'd already started to amend the policy to read that employees may date and develop friendships and relationships with other employees—both inside and outside of the workplace—as long as those relationships don't have a negative impact on their work or the work of others.

The older man scrutinized Dwayne. "You really care about my daughter."

"I want to marry her...with your permission, of course." Dwayne's father would be proud of him for remembering the lessons he'd taught Dwayne and Dwight about women and relationships. And he hoped Mr. Townsend didn't have any objections because he planned to ask Valencia to be his wife, regardless.

Mr. Townsend leaned forward and clasped his hands.

"You've been dating Valencia for only four months. You think that's enough time to decide on marriage?"

"Absolutely. This is not something I take lightly, Mr. Townsend. As I said before, I love Valencia and I will protect and care for her for as long as I draw breath."

He scrutinized Dwayne a long moment, then finally nodded. "Then you have my blessing, son."

Dwayne released a deep breath. "Thank you. I plan to propose to her tomorrow at my parent's house and I would like for you and Mrs. Townsend to be there."

He lifted a brow. "So soon?"

"I want to start the new year off right."

"I see. Well, if your parents don't mind."

"They won't mind at all." Or at least they wouldn't once Dwayne called tonight to let them know. His mother was going to be ecstatic, since she'd been trying to marry him and his brother off for the past few years.

"Then we'll be there."

He gave Mr. Townsend the address and time. "Can you wait until we leave to tell Mrs. Townsend? I want it to be a surprise."

"The way my wife is, I'm probably going to wait until I'm pulling up in your parent's driveway before I say anything. That way, she won't have time to let anything slip," Mr. Townsend said with a laugh.

The two men shared a smile and shook hands. Valencia and her mother returned a moment later with a tray holding slices of pound cake. Dwayne ate his cake and enjoyed getting to know Valencia's parents. Afterwards, he thanked them and citing wanting to have Valencia home before the New Year's shooting began, they left.

"What did my father say to you?" Valencia asked as soon as he got into the car.

He chuckled. "Relax, Lyn. He just wanted to know the usual Dad info when a guy is dating his daughter."

"He was smiling when we came back, so I guess it didn't go too bad."

"Not at all. I think your parents are great. And I know my parents are going to love you."

"I hope so."

They got back to her place a few minutes before midnight.

"Do you mind if I change clothes?" Valencia asked the moment they hit the door. "I need to get out of this dress and these heels."

"Go right ahead." It would give him time to call his mother. He waited until he heard her close the bathroom door and pulled out his phone. "Hey, Mom," he said when she picked up.

"Hi, sweetheart. Happy New Year five minutes early."

Dwayne laughed. "Happy New Year to you. Do you mind if I invite a couple of people over tomorrow?"

"Dwayne, I've told you guys every year you can invite your friends. And I hope at least one of those people is a woman."

"Yes, one is a woman."

"Hallelujah!"

"I'll see you tomorrow, Mom."

"Bye, son."

He shook his head and disconnected. A thought came to him. He scrolled down his favorites list and hit the call button again.

"Hey."

"Hey, bro. I need a favor." Dwayne told Dwight what he needed and his brother readily agreed. "Thanks."

"No problem. Later."

He ended the call just before Valencia returned wearing a pair of comfortable sweats and long-sleeved tee.

"Whew. I feel so much better now." She dropped down on the sofa next to him and clicked on the TV. They caught the ball in its final minute.

They counted down together. "Happy New Year, baby." He kissed her deeply.

"Same to you."

He handed her the box.

"Exactly how many of these did you buy?" She shook her head, but was smiling. "I don't know about you." She opened the box and gasped softly. "Dwayne, this is…"

"Yes, the key to my heart." He'd given her a heart key as the final charm.

She launched herself at him, knocking him backwards on the sofa. "I love you!"

"I love you, too," he said, laughing.

Valencia sat up slightly. "So…about the whole starting the new year as friends thing…I was just playing. I want to start the new year just like this."

Her words were music to his ears. "Ditto, baby."

She started unbuttoning his shirt. "So, about those plans I mentioned during dinner…"

"I'm all yours."

"Yes, you are."

Dwayne groaned as her tongue made a path across his chest. He agreed. He wanted to start every day of every year in just this way. For the rest of his life.

CHAPTER 6

"*W*hat if his family doesn't like me?" Valencia said as she applied lipstick.

Leah rolled her eyes. "Girl, they're going to love you. Quit being so dramatic."

She glanced at Leah's frowning face on her iPad. "I'm just nervous. We went from dating in secret to meet-the-parents in a blink of an eye. I still can't believe how he charmed my parents." And she laughed every time she thought about her mother's response.

"In my opinion, the guys have a harder time because they have to win over a girl's father. All you have to do is smile, offer to take a couple of dishes to the table or help clean up and you're in."

Valencia laughed. "Anybody with home training would offer to do that, so I don't think that's a good measure." She picked up the iPad and went back into the bedroom for her shoes. Dwayne had told her to dress casually and, after a good thirty minutes of discarding one outfit after another, she'd settled on a pair of ivory jeans and matching off-the shoulder sweater, and her brown ankle boots.

"Hey, it can't hurt. What time is the get-together?"

"Dwayne made it sound like it's an all-day kind of thing. He should be here to pick me up in about half an hour."

"By the way, I looked him up and *Lawd, have mercy*! The man is fine, fine, *fine*. You said he had a brother."

"He does. An *identical twin* brother."

Leah's eyes widened and her mouth dropped. "There are two of them?"

Valencia smiled and nodded. Her doorbell rang. "Hang on. There's someone at my door," she said walking toward the front. "It's probably my neighbor. She promised me some of her 7-Up cake."

"Ooh, the one you let me taste last Christmas?"

"Yep."

"Girl, you'd better save me a piece."

She laughed. "You know I've got—" She looked through the peephole and saw Dwayne standing there and quickly opened the door. "Dwayne. You're early."

"I know. I couldn't wait to see you." Dwayne slid an arm around her waist and crushed his mouth against hers in a greedy, demanding kiss.

"*Hellooooo!* I'm still here."

Valencia tore her mouth away. "Oh, my goodness. I forgot I'm on FaceTime with my friend. Sorry, Leah."

"Yeah, yeah. All that moaning and groaning is making a sistah jealous."

Dwayne laughed and eased the iPad from Valencia's hand. "Hey, Leah. I'm Dwayne. It's nice to meet you."

"Same here. I heard you have a brother. He's not married, is he?"

"*Leah!* Really?" Valencia snatched the iPad back.

"What? I'm just asking."

Dwayne leaned over. "He's single and so are a few of my cousins. The family is having a little something at my parent's house today and you're welcome to join us if you don't have any pla—."

"Oh, *nooo*, I am totally free."

"Great." He gave her the address. "Valencia and I are heading over now."

"They're only fifteen minutes from me, so I'll meet you there."

Valencia stared at her friend doing a little shimmy dance. The grin on Leah's face was so wide, it barely fit in the screen. "I'll see you in a little while, wild woman." She ended the call. "That was really nice of you to invite her. Are you sure your parents won't mind?"

"Positive. By the way, you look absolutely gorgeous." His gaze made a slow path down her body and back up. "I think I'm going enjoy peeling those jeans off you."

Her pulse skipped and her core throbbed in anticipation. She cleared her throat. "Thanks. You don't look so bad yourself." Dressed in all black, the man looked good enough to eat. "Let me get my jacket and purse."

Laughing with Dwayne about Leah had taken her mind off meeting his family, but her nervousness returned the moment he took her hand and led her up his parent's driveway. The two-story house was located on a tree-lined street with stately homes and immaculately manicured lawns, and overlooked the hills. He unlocked the door and gestured her forward. She stepped inside and didn't know where to settle her gaze first—the highly polished wood floors in the foyer leading to an elegantly furnished living room with deep tan plush carpeting, the vaulted ceilings, or the formal dining room off to the left holding a table with seating for ten. "This is gorgeous. I see where you get your taste from now." It reminded her of Dwayne's four-bedroom house. She'd fallen in love with his place the first time he'd taken her there.

He smiled. "I let my mom and sister do the decorating."

"I thought I heard voices."

Valencia turned and met the smiling face of an older woman with features so reminiscent of Dwayne's she had to be his mother.

"Hey, Mom." Dwayne bent and kissed her cheek. He introduced Valencia.

"It's an honor to meet you, Mrs. Albright. You have a beautiful home."

"Thank you. And I'm *very* happy to meet you, Valencia. Please make yourself comfortable. We're all in the family room and patio."

All of a sudden, Valencia heard thundering footsteps. Then two boys who looked to be around six or seven came barreling around the corner. They were twins, Valencia realized.

"Uncle Dwayne!" they chorused, launching themselves at Dwayne, and tackling him to the ground.

"You can't hold me down," Dwayne said, wrestling and growling with them.

"Yes, we can."

Mrs. Albright shook her head. "At thirty-six, he still rolls around on the ground like he did when he was six."

Valencia couldn't do anything but laugh. She'd never seen this side of Dwayne, but the sight touched her heart and she instinctively knew he'd be a great father.

"*Jalen Allen McCall* and *Justin Aaron McCall*, get off your uncle!"

The boys froze and so did Valencia. She spun around and saw a frowning chocolate-skinned woman with her hands on her hips.

"Aw, come on, Shelby," Dwayne said. "We're just having fun." He ruffled the boys' hair, then stood with them in his arms. "Valencia, this is my baby sister, Shelby. And, as you heard—and everybody else in the neighborhood—these are my nephews."

An embarrassed look crossed Shelby's face. "I'm sorry. Hi, Valencia. Nice to meet you."

She divided a speculative glance between Dwayne and Valencia and Valencia wondered what it meant. "Nice to meet you, too, Shelby. Your sons are adorable."

Shelby shook her head. "Rambunctious is more like it. And this one here," she said, playfully shoving Dwayne, "makes it worse."

Dwayne dropped a kiss on his sister's temple and set the twins on their feet. "Party pooper." He took Valencia's hand and followed his mother to the back of the house where music and laughter greeted them.

The laughter and conversation stopped abruptly when they saw Valencia. She wanted to hide. A man, who she assumed to be Dwayne's father, came over and draped his arm around his wife's shoulder. "Who do we have here, Phyllis?"

The smiles they shared reminded Valencia of her parents.

"Dad. I'd like you to meet Valencia Townsend."

"Welcome to our home, Valencia."

"Thank you. It's nice to meet you."

"Alright, everybody," Dwayne called out. "This beautiful woman is Valencia Townsend. For all my single cousins, she's mine. That means a polite hello and a handshake. That's it."

Laughter broke out and a few of them yelled out comments.

"You're lucky you said something."

"I guarantee she'll like me better."

Valencia placed her hand on her hip. "Are you out of your mind?"

"Yep. Out of my mind in love with you."

She had no comeback for that one. A young woman dressed to kill in a body-hugging red dress, shot Valencia a glare and stormed out of the room. She opened her mouth to ask Dwayne about it and her cell chimed. She dug it out of her pocket and read the text from her friend. "Leah is outside."

"Okay."

They went to let her in and another round of introductions ensued.

Leah whispered to Valencia, "Girl, there are so many fine men here."

"Yes, there are." But she only had eyes for one. She chatted with his sister and brother-in-law for a few minutes, then Dwight came over.

"How's it going, Valencia?"

"Good. You have a big family."

Dwight glanced around the room. "We do. I've never seen my brother so happy. Whatever you're doing, don't stop." A grin tilted the corner of his mouth.

His smile took her by surprise and softened the usually hard lines bracketing his handsome face. "He makes me happy, too."

"I know you're not over here hitting on my woman." Dwayne draped an arm around Valencia's shoulder and kissed her temple.

Dwight just shook his head and walked away.

"You two must have done that to a lot of girls growing up."

"I plead the fifth," he said with a straight face.

Valencia laughed.

"Let's go outside on the deck for a minute."

They left through the kitchen's sliding glass door and stood at the railing overlooking a huge backyard with a gated in pool on one side and outdoor kitchen on the other. The temperatures had warmed to the sixties, so it wasn't too cold.

Dwayne stood behind her with his arms around her waist. "Your family is off the hook." The love that flowed between them was evident.

"We are a lively bunch, but I wouldn't trade any of them for the world."

Valencia glanced up at him over her shoulder. "And the woman in the red dress?"

"Her name's Leticia and she's a family friend. I've known her practically all my life and she's like a sister. In fact, she and Shelby are best friends."

"Does she know that?" She recalled the hurt and angry look on the woman's face.

"Yes. I've never led her to believe that she was anything but a friend. I'm sure she'll be okay after I talk to her."

She doubted it would be that easy, but since he knew the woman better, she'd let him deal with it. They fell silent and she was content to stand there with him. She didn't know how much time had passed before he stepped back.

"Valencia."

She shifted slightly and he dropped down to one knee. Her heart started pounding so hard, she thought she would pass out. He held the same colored box as the other gifts, but this one was smaller. He opened it to reveal a princess cut diamond solitaire that had to be at least two carats surrounded by two rows of baguettes. *Yep, I'm going to pass out.*

"I don't even know where to begin sharing the feelings in my heart. If you could see inside, you'd find a depth of passion and a love so strong it overwhelms me. Nothing in my life means as much as you, Lyn. You are my missing piece, the better part of me, my everything. I want to spend all my midnight moments with you from now until eternity. Will you marry me?"

Valencia barely let him finish the words before she yelled,

"*Yes!*" She was crying and bouncing up and down as he put the ring on her finger. Dwayne stood, swung her up in his arms and kissed her with a passion she felt through her entire body. A roaring cheer went up, startling her. She whipped her head around and saw everyone crowded in the door. Leah was crying and pumping her fist in the air. "*Mom? Dad?*" She stared questioningly at Dwayne.

He shrugged. "I talked to your father last night."

"You planned all this?"

Dwayne nodded.

"I can't...I don't even have words right now." Her emotions welled up with such force, she couldn't utter a word.

"As long as you're happy, that's all that matters."

When she finally found her voice, she asked, "So, when do you want to do this?"

"Today works for me."

"*Today?*" Once again, she found herself momentarily speechless. "We can't get married today. Don't we need blood tests, a license, or something? And who's going to perform the ceremony?"

"We don't need blood tests, we can petition to get an amended marriage certificate since we don't have a license, and we can have a bigger ceremony later. As far as someone to perform the ceremony...I've got that covered. So, what do you say?"

Valencia's head was spinning. When Dwayne said he was done with all the secrecy, evidently, he meant every word. *It's not like you don't want to be married to the man, so why are you hesitating?* her inner voice asked.

"Did I point out the two benefits to saying yes?"

"What benefits?"

"Two wedding nights and two honeymoons."

That sealed it for her. "Well, since you put it that way,

there's no need to let all this winter white I'm wearing go to waste. Let's do it!" Their families cheered again.

Dwayne threw his head back and laughed. "Uncle Gene, are you ready?"

A man stepped outside with a small book in his hand.

Valencia's gaze flew to Dwayne's.

"Sweetheart, I'd like to introduce you to Judge Eugene Albright."

His uncle chuckled. "Valencia, you'll learn that in this family, we don't do anything by half."

"I see."

"All we need is a maid of honor and best man and we'll be set," Dwayne said, gesturing for Leah and his twin.

Once the two attendants took their places, Valencia and Dwayne spoke their vows. The love she had for this man overflowed in her heart and she couldn't stop crying. She'd found her soulmate and she looked forward to every one of their midnight moments. From now until eternity.

OTHER BOOKS IN THE SERIES

New Year Bae-Solutions Series

Turn the page for a peek into my latest release!

Staring forty in the face, Braxton Harper is accustomed to having everything in his life fall into its precise place. Only he hasn't found that special one and he refuses to settle for anything less than a woman who is his perfect match. The moment Londyn Grant dances into his life, Braxton is convinced he's found her. Kiss by sizzling kiss, the sexy doctor slowly lets her guard down. Now, if she'd only let him into her heart...

Londyn knows heartbreak. By day, the psychologist counsels others, but she has yet to find a way to heal her own heart. The last thing she wants is another relationship. However, sensual and sensitive Braxton tempts her to open up and, for the first time in her life, she's letting passion rule. But it's going to take a little therapeutic intervention—in and out of the bedroom—to get Londyn to see that this time she's found the real thing.

DO ME EXCERPT

Ugh! I hate weddings. Londyn Grant moved back as far as the crowded dance floor allowed, but it still didn't create enough space between her and her dance partner. The mixture of cologne, smoke and alcohol was enough to make her nauseous. She couldn't believe she was the only one from the office here. Her coworkers—all five of them—had backed out of attending the wedding at the last minute, citing one reason or another and leaving Londyn as the only attendee at their administrative assistant's daughter's nuptials. Her sole reason for accepting the invitation had been because she had counted on having her two male colleagues to create a buffer between her and the constant flow of wannabee suitors. She had declined several of the celebrations over the past year because she'd begun feel to like prey in a nightclub, as if she wore a neon sign posted on her forehead that read, *single and lonely*. Okay, so that might have been the truth, but since her disastrous relationship ended a couple of years ago, she'd crossed men off her list. She'd take loneliness over a broken heart any day.

Another song came on and the man raised his hands in

the air and did a spin move. Londyn took advantage, and while he had his back turned, snuck off the dance floor. Fanning herself, she headed to the bar for something cool. Out of her periphery she noticed a man dancing with a teen. Her steps slowed and she stood transfixed by his movements. He seemed to be enjoying himself, if the smile on his face was any indication. Tall, rich, brown skin with close-cropped dark hair, a beard riding his jaw like a shadow—giving his handsome face a dangerous edge—and a smile that would probably make the strongest sister weak. He'd discarded his suit jacket and even in the white dress shirt, she could tell he had a fabulous body. Yeah. Sexy. Londyn shook herself. *What am I doing? No men,* she reminded herself as she continued to her destination.

Minutes later, Corinne came toward her with a wide grin befitting a proud mother of the bride. "Oh, Londyn, thank you for coming." They shared a quick hug.

"It was a beautiful ceremony and they look so happy." She'd spoken with the bride and groom briefly to offer congratulations.

"Wasn't it? I'm so excited for them. My baby girl has married into a wonderful family. They're all so warm and friendly. Have you had a chance to meet some of our family?" She winked at Londyn and whispered conspiratorially, "Quite a few of these handsome devils are single from what I understand. My nephew just moved here from Florida. He's joining a law practice here. I could introduce y—"

"No," Londyn said quickly. She forced a smile. "I mean, I'll just mingle for a while, if you don't mind." She didn't do match-making, either. "I'll probably only stay a little longer."

"Okay, but let me know if you change your mind."

She wanted to tell the woman she didn't plan to change her mind in this century or the next, but kept the comment to herself.

"I'd better go. My sister needs something. If I don't talk to you before you leave, I'll see you on Monday." Corinne rushed off.

Thank goodness," Londyn muttered. She went back to her assigned table and sipped her ginger ale while the party continued in full swing. The DJ played a mixture of old and new school songs that had everyone either up on the floor or bobbing their heads in their seats. This was how she had envisioned her own wedding—full of love, laughter and the promise of forever. Tears burned her eyes and the old sadness bubbled up inside her, but she forced it back down. She refused to shed another tear over her ex. *The jerk.*

She continued to scan the room, smiling at a senior couple out on the dance floor grooving to Usher's "Yeah!" Eventually, everyone relinquished the floor to them and let out a series of whoops when the woman did a little shimmy.

"Go, Grandma!" a woman called out.

Everyone around the room had gotten into the action, except the man she'd seen dancing earlier. He sat a table with a heavy scowl lining his face. She wondered why. Maybe she wasn't the only one who hated weddings. Curiosity got the better of her —as a psychologist, she had an interest in human behavior—and she found herself crossing the spacious ballroom to his table.

"I thought I was the only one who hated weddings."

He glanced up at her and slowly rose to his feet. "Why would a beautiful woman like you hate weddings?"

"Probably for the same reason you do."

He lifted a brow. "Is your mother so determined to marry you off that she's bringing a string of guys around and letting them know you're single?"

"Not quite, but they've been coming anyway. May I?" Londyn asked, gesturing to the empty chair next to his. She'd spent the past two years telling herself she neither wanted or needed a man, that she had no time in her busy schedule for romance. She had devised so many excuses that she'd become adept at keeping any and every man at bay. Yet, tonight, she had purposely sought one out. A man whose mother thought he needed help. Men who looked like him didn't stay unattached long and could take his pick among women. Just from his mannerisms he seemed to be a good catch. She couldn't recall any man she'd dated standing at her approach. So why, she wondered, wasn't he seeing anyone?

"Please." He seated her then reclaimed his chair.

"Braxton." He extended his hand. "And you are?"

His large hand closed around her smaller one. *Strong and warm.* And since he seemingly wasn't interested in relationships, safe. "Londyn. Bride or groom's family?"

"Groom. He's my cousin. What about you?"

"Bride. A member of the family is my colleague."

Braxton opened his mouth, then closed it. His lips settled into a grim line.

Londyn followed his gaze and saw a woman she assumed to be his mother, a look of determination on her face, approaching with another woman. She chuckled.

He hopped to his feet. "Would you like to dance, Londyn?" She read the plea in his eyes. "Sure. I'll help you out."

A slow grin curved his lips. "I appreciate it."

He led her out to the dance floor. Belatedly she realized the DJ had switched from the fast-paced dance songs to a slow, jazzy ballad. The moment Braxton wrapped his arms around her, she knew she'd made a mistake. He smelled good and his hard body against hers felt even better. Even in her heels, he towered over her five-foot, three-inch frame by almost a foot. He gathered her closer, keeping a respectable distance, but his thighs brushed against hers and she stifled a moan. All the emotions she'd repressed since her breakup surfaced, and for the first time in a very long while, she felt desire. Londyn was torn between wanting to flee or move closer to the man whom she now realized was anything but safe.

"So, what do you propose I do as payment?"

She looked up at him. "Payment?"

"For helping me."

Londyn averted her gaze. "Nothing, since you're helping me, too," she said without thought. She wanted to snatch the words back as soon as they left her mouth.

ABOUT THE AUTHOR

Sheryl Lister is a multi-award-winning author and has enjoyed reading and writing for as long as she can remember. She is a former pediatric occupational therapist with over twenty years of experience, and resides in California. Sheryl is a wife, mother of three daughters and a son-in-love, and grandmother to two special little boys. When she's not writing, Sheryl can be found on a date with her husband or in the kitchen creating appetizers. For more information, visit her website at www.sheryllister.com.

facebook.com/sheryllisterauthor
twitter.com/1Slynne
instagram.com/sheryllister

Never Letting Go (Carnivale Chronicles)

Embracing Ever After (Once Upon a Baby #1)

Do Me (Irresistible Husband)